MONSTER HUNTER

WEREWOLF

STEVE BARLOW AND STEVE SKIDMORE

ILLUSTRATED BY PAUL DAVIDSON

Franklin Watts
First published in Great Britain in 2018
by The Watts Publishing Group

Text © Steve Barlow and Steve Skidmore 2018
Illustrations © The Watts Publishing Group 2018
Design: Cathryn Gilbert
Executive editor: Adrian Cole

ISBN 978 1 4451 5942 3
ebook ISBN 978 1 4451 5943 0
Library ebook ISBN 978 1 4451 5944 7

1 3 5 7 9 10 8 6 4 2

Printed in Great Britain

MIX
Paper from
responsible sources
FSC® C104740
www.fsc.org

Franklin Watts
An imprint of
Hachette Children's Group
Part of The Watts Publishing Group
Carmelite House
50 Victoria Embankment
London EC4Y 0DZ

An Hachette UK Company
www.hachette.co.uk

www.franklinwatts.co.uk

Mission Statement

You are the hero of this mission.

Each section of this book is numbered. At the end of most sections, you will have to make a choice. The choice you make will take you to a different section of the book.

Some of your choices will help you to complete your mission successfully. But if you make the wrong choice, death may be the best you can hope for! Because even that is better than being UNDEAD and becoming a slave of the monsters you have sworn to destroy!

Dare you go up against a world of monsters?

All right, then.

Let's see what you've got...

Introduction

You are an agent of **G.H.O.S.T.** — Global Headquarters Opposing Supernatural Threats.

Our world is under constant attack by supernatural horrors that lurk in the shadows. It's your job to make sure they stay there.

You have studied all kinds of monsters, and know their habits and behaviour. You are an master of disguise, able to move among monsters in human form as a spy. You are an expert in all forms of martial arts. G.H.O.S.T. has supplied you with weapons, equipment and other assets that make you capable of destroying any supernatural creature.

G.H.O.S.T.

You are based at Arcane Hall, a spooky mansion. Your butler, Cranberry, is another G.H.O.S.T. agent who assists you in your adventures, providing you with information and backup.

Your life at Arcane Hall is comfortable and peaceful; but you know that at any moment, the G.H.O.S.T. High Command can order you into action in any part of the world...

Go to 1.

1

Cranberry's voice crackles in your ear. "How's the trip going?"

You stare out of the windscreen of the hired Lada 4x4. "I never want to see snow, cabbage soup or birch trees, ever again."

"Sorry," says Cranberry cheerfully, "but the Russian government doesn't like G.H.O.S.T."

"So no Phantom Flyer and no Spook Truck? All I've got is a few bits of basic equipment that are not going to be much help if I have to fight werewolves."

"You shouldn't have to," says Cranberry. "Werewolves are mostly shy, and avoid human contact. They hunt animals, just like ordinary wolves. Their bite infects humans with the were-virus and turns them into werewolves. But we have a treaty with them; they don't bite people unless they're trapped and desperate."

"Then what am I doing in Siberia?"

"There's been a sudden increase in werewolf attacks in the taiga. Werewolf leaders are worried that hotheads they can't control are on the rampage."

"And G.H.O.S.T. thinks there's a connection with the Wolf Conservation Project run by Professor Fedorov?"

"Your first move is to meet Fedorov, and find out. Be careful — he has a short fuse."

You arrive at the gates of a compound. An unsmiling guard checks your ID and directs you to a wooden shack labelled ADMIN BUILDING.

The moment you step out of your car, a great white wolf comes bounding across the snow, making straight for you!

To use your WOW gun, go to 13.

To use your HOWL detector, go to 27.

2

The colonel shakes your hand. "I am beginning to see the point of co-operating with G.H.O.S.T." He leads you to a Ural Typhoon armoured all-terrain vehicle. "Can I offer you a lift?"

As the truck bounces over forest tracks, the colonel's radio operator gets through to Cranberry.

"Glad you made it, Agent," he says when you have explained recent events. "Our sensors show the werewolf pack is heading east. Other packs are moving in the same direction — they seem to be making for Lake Baikal."

You tell this news to the colonel. He nods and speaks urgently into the radio.

"My superiors are willing to help you deal with the werewolves," he says at length. "Will you follow them in this vehicle — or by helicopter?"

To go by road, go to 21.

To use the helicopter, go to 36.

3

You try to follow the pack, but you are soon lost in the dense forest. Before long you skid into a tree and the car overturns in the snow.

You struggle out to find yourself surrounded by werewolves. They leap to the attack, snarling and biting.

You feel the were-virus spread through your body as the terrible transformation to werewolf begins!

It's snow joke! Go back to 1.

4

A "skidder" machine has a log in its grapple, ready to drop onto the carriage truck. You release the log and it falls onto the werewolf, pinning it to the carriage.

You start the machine, sending the log towards the whirring saw blade. Werewolves heal quickly but not when they've been sawn in half!

You head for the door, but before you reach it, a group of Russian soldiers bursts in, firing over their shoulders. You can guess what is after them.

"Over here!" you cry.

The startled soldiers hesitate — and some of them swing their guns to aim at you!

To run from the soldiers, go to 25.

To ask them for help, go to 10.

5

Abandoning the truck, you and Yuri run across the ice. But swift shadows close in. Soon you are surrounded by werewolves.

You fight valiantly, but the odds against you are overwhelming. Both you and Yuri fall to the fangs and claws of your enemies.

You've been put on ice! Go back to 1.

You point at the captive creatures. "Professor, those are werewolves!"

Fedorov's eyes widen. "Madness!" he cries. "Werewolves don't exist! You want to close my project down. Guards!" Uniformed men arrive, unslinging their weapons. "See that this foreigner leaves — immediately!"

Soon you are driving away from the compound, but you don't go far. As darkness falls, you leave the car hidden in a clump of trees and make your way back on foot.

But you soon realise you are being followed. The werewolves are out — and they're hunting you!

Go to 33.

You head for the snowmobile, only to find that it has been smashed to pieces by the werewolves.

You raise your WOW gun as the creatures pour from every quarter of the camp. "There are too many of them! How come this thing doesn't have an 'automatic' mode?"

"Are you crazy?" asks Cranberry. "It fires silver darts. Do you think we're made of money?"

To run into the forest, go to 17.

To stand and fight the werewolves, go to 31.

"That's too long," you tell the general, "and your troops are not trained or equipped to fight werewolves."

Cranberry's voice breaks in from the radio.

"I suggest you contact Yuri Paulenko. He used to be with G.H.O.S.T. He works in mining these days, but he knows all about werewolves." He gives you Paulenko's address — a fishing village on the shores of Lake Baikal.

An army jeep takes you there. Yuri is not pleased at being disturbed — especially by you.

"Werewolves killed my family," he rages. "And G.H.O.S.T. did nothing to stop them. Leave me alone!"

To threaten Yuri, go to 16.

To try to persuade him, go to 28.

You throw yourself into the back of the truck.

"Go!"

Yuri revs the engine, reverses onto the ice and sends the truck into a skid-turn. He races away across the frozen lake. Angry werewolves stream after the truck.

To use Yuri's explosive charges against them, go to 38.

To fight them off with Yuri's WOW and VCB, go to 19.

10

You raise your hands. "Hold your fire! I'm a friend."

A man in a colonel's uniform steps forward.

"What are you doing here?" he demands in English.

"Investigating werewolves," you tell him.

The colonel looks uneasy. "There are no such things!"

"Then what were you and your men firing at out there?" you demand.

The colonel frowns. "We received a report that this mill was being attacked — and three of my men have disappeared. You had better tell me what you know."

You tell the colonel your story. He listens attentively.

"Supposing you are right," he says at length, "how do we fight these creatures?"

"Not with guns," you tell the colonel. "Not unless they fire silver bullets."

The colonel stares. "Silver bullets?"

"Forget it," you say. "If you and your men want to survive, do exactly as I say."

To lead the soldiers in an attack on the werewolves, go to 49.

To use the mill equipment to fight them, go to 29.

11

The sawmill seems deserted, but you hear the noise of a generator powering the lights and machinery.

A workman appears. He has heavy eyebrows that meet across his nose, long curved fingernails and low-set, pointed ears.

He says something in Russian. You don't understand the words but he seems to be asking for help.

To go with the man, go to 20.

To ignore his plea, go to 35.

12

As you take the unconscious Yuri by the shoulders, the Vurdalak grabs you from behind.

"I will gather more followers," he snarls. "You will never defeat me."

He raises you high above his head and hurls you into the freezing waters of the lake. Your body goes into shock: you are about to share the fate of the werewolves you have destroyed.

You nearly made it — but that's cold comfort! Go back to 1.

13

You snatch the WOW gun from your briefcase and fire a silver dart into the wolf's chest. The creature skids to a halt. It licks its wound and whines. You are puzzled — the silver in the dart should have finished off a werewolf straight away.

A bearded man erupts from the building. He is furious. "What are you doing?" he demands.

"Professor Fedorov?" you ask. "I was protecting myself from this wolf..."

"Wolf?" roars the professor. "Idiot! That's my pet Samoyed dog, Boris!"

Brushing aside your apologies, the professor orders you to leave. Guards arrive to see that you obey.

You drive out through the gate — but as soon as you are out of sight of the compound, you leave the car hidden in a clump of trees. As darkness falls, you make your way back on foot.

You have not gone far when you see swift shapes flitting between the snow-covered trees. You are being followed!

Go to 33.

14

You fight on, but it is soon clear that there is no hope. All around you, your little army is torn to pieces by ravening werewolves.

Your own fate is worse — you are captured and bitten. You feel the were-virus coursing through your veins. You will soon join the ranks of your enemies.

W(h)ere can you turn at a moment like this? Back to 1!

15

You fire a wolfsbane-tipped bolt from your VCB at the werewolf, killing it instantly.

You check the body for ID and find a dog tag ("What else?" you mutter) that identifies your victim as one of the werewolf leaders who called G.H.O.S.T. for help.

Cranberry is scathing. "Nice work, Agent! You've just killed an ally!"

Cursing, you return to the snowmobile — but at the same moment, the lights of the camp go out. In the darkness, you sense unseen forms closing in on you.

Go to 33.

16

You take out a gun borrowed from your Russian hosts. "You have no choice!"

Cursing, Yuri leaps at you. In the struggle, the gun goes off. A terrible impact jars your body. You sink to the floor, mortally wounded.

You should have asked nicely! Go back to 1.

17

You crash through the trees, expecting the pack to catch up with you at any moment.

But a check with your HOWL detector reveals that the main pack has stayed in the camp. The bad news is that three werewolves in wolf-man form are heading your way.

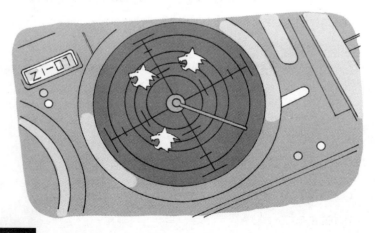

To use your **WOW gun** on your attackers, go to **41**.

To use your **VCB**, go to **26**.

To fight them hand-to-hand, go to **45**.

18

You fall behind the professor and use your comms link to tell Cranberry what you have discovered.

"You must destroy the werewolves, Agent," he says. "But don't put them on their guard. Your WOW gun is noisy. Even firing your VCB will be heard by a werewolf's sensitive ears. And remember that werewolves can appear in three forms; wolf, human and wolf-man, the most dangerous of all!"

You look up. Night is falling, and in darkness, the werewolves will have the advantage. You decide to wait for morning.

"It's getting late," you tell the professor. "Can you put me up for the night?"

He scowls. "There's a camp bed in the admin office."

You head back for the office and find a comfortless bed. You lie on it to reread your briefing notes.

The door bursts in. Three werewolves in wolf-man form charge into the room.

But you are prepared for a sneak attack. You twitch aside the blankets, bring up your WOW gun and fire. The first wolf-man drops lifeless to the floor. The others flee. Slinging your VCB across your back, you follow them outside.

To chase the wolf-men, go to 37.

To warn Professor Fedorov, go to 47.

19

You fire a stream of darts and crossbow bolts into your pursuers, destroying many. But on the ice, the werewolves are as swift as the truck. Soon, wolves are leaping into the back and transforming into wolf-men. One smashes the rear window of the cab and attacks Yuri, who loses control. The truck turns over, throwing you both out onto the ice.

Go to 5.

20

The man points towards a tumbledown shack and speaks again.

You make for the shack, passing close to the man. As soon as your back is turned, you hear a snarling sound behind you. You turn and stare in horror. The man was a werewolf in human form — and you missed the classic signs!

The creature turns into a wolf-man and lunges for your unprotected throat.

You've not been paying attention! Check out the description of a disguised werewolf in Section 47: then go back to 1.

21

"We'll follow them by road," you say.

The colonel orders the driver to increase speed. But this is more easily said than done. The forest tracks are winding and rutted. Several times the powerful truck gets bogged down and has to be winched out of mud-holes.

You realise that this way, you will never catch up with the swift-running werewolves.

Go to 48.

22

You unsling your VCB and point it at the professor. "Stay where you are."

But Fedorov lashes out, catching you unawares, and escapes.

You follow Fedorov's footprints, and find him unlocking the gate of the werewolves' enclosure.

"He shan't kill you!" he screams. "Run! Run!"

But the werewolves' blood is up. Before your horrified eyes, they turn on the professor and tear him apart.

You fire VCB bolts into the pack. Several fall. The rest storm the main gate, overpowering the guards. They break down the gate and stream through, out into the night.

To follow the wolves on Professor Fedorov's snowmobile, go to 39.

To follow them in your car, go to 3.

23

You explain your plan to Yuri, with Cranberry listening in via Yuri's comms link.

"I'd call that a terrible plan," Cranberry says, "if I could think of a better one."

"Must we give the Vurdalak the chance to surrender?" asks Yuri.

"Yes," you say, "because of the treaty."

Yuri shrugs. "He'll refuse." He drives the truck down a steep bank and onto the frozen lake. The ice is thawing and turning slushy.

"I'm not sure this will bear the weight of the truck," you tell Yuri.

To drive on, go to 32.

To leave the truck, go to 5.

24

You take a silver choke-chain from your belt pouch and loop it around the werewolf's neck.

He gasps with pain. "Stop! I am on your side."

You loosen the chain. "Convince me."

"I am one of those who called G.H.O.S.T. in. Our council discovered that renegade werewolves had taken over Professor Fedorov's project. They have a new leader called the Vurdalak, who is summoning all the werewolf packs in Siberia to a wolfmoot. He plans to rise up against humans and turn them into werewolf slaves!" He looks around nervously. "It is not safe to stay here..."

"Not for you, traitor!" From out of the shadows, a werewolf in wolf-man form steps forward, howling. More werewolves surge forward and pounce on your luckless ally.

To run for the snowmobile, go to 7.

To stand and fight, go to 31.

25

You turn to run from the soldiers. Maybe they think you are a werewolf, too. Maybe they are just trigger-happy. They open fire.

You feel the hammer-blow impact of the bullets and fall to the sawdust-covered floor. At least this way, you won't become a werewolf.

It's not much consolation.

You can't outrun a bullet. Go back to 1.

26

You take a flashlight from your pocket. Holding it in one hand, you fire your VCB at the wolf-men.

You take out two — but you miss with your third shot. The wolf-man steps behind a tree and gives a deafening howl. You hear the rush of hundreds of paws on the snow as the rest of the werewolf pack speeds to his aid.

Go to 31.

You swiftly point your HOWL detector at the creature. The screen remains blank. You realise that this isn't a wolf; it's a Samoyed. The dog bounds around you, barking happily.

A snowmobile appears. The bearded man riding it stops and kills the engine.

"Boris seems to like you," he says. "I, however, dislike interference."

"I'll try not to be a nuisance," you tell him. "Perhaps you could show me around?"

The professor grunts and leads you to a large enclosure surrounded by a strong chain-link fence. Wolves are prowling inside. "The packs in the taiga are in decline," he growls. "We are breeding a new population to boost their numbers..."

But you are hardly listening. A quick glance at your HOWL detector has confirmed your worst fears. The creatures in the enclosure are not wolves — they are werewolves.

To tell the professor what you have discovered, go to 6.

To consult Cranberry, go to 18.

To shoot the werewolves, go to 43.

You glare at Yuri. "I need your help but I won't beg for it. I'm offering you a chance to avenge your family."

Yuri scowls. "Tell me what is happening."

You explain that the werewolf clans are converging on Lake Baikal for a wolfmoot with their new leader, the Vurdalak.

Yuri considers. "I still have my old equipment: you're welcome to share it. But before we start a war, I want to talk to the leader of the local clan."

To agree, go to 46.

To refuse, go to 40.

29

You decide you must divide your forces. While your group engages the werewolves, the colonel's makes for the great kiln-drying oven where the sawn planks are cured.

You hold the werewolves at bay as long as you can. Then you break off the fight and head towards the drying oven. You run between rows of planks that smell strongly of petrol and diesel fuel. The colonel's men, emptying the last of the fuel onto the logs, drop their cans and join you as you sprint out of the back door — just as the werewolves enter at the front.

The colonel raises a flare gun and fires a round into the fuel-soaked planks. Instantly, his men slam the door shut. More men emerge from hiding to shut and bar the front doors.

The werewolves are trapped in a gigantic oven full of burning timber. They won't be troubling you again!

Go to 2.

30

You leap from the cab and fire the VCB you have borrowed from Yuri. Two of the werewolves fall.

"Stop, you idiot!" cries Yuri as other wolf-men rip the driver's door from its hinges. They drag him from the vehicle and tear him to pieces.

You keep firing until all the werewolves are dead — but so is Yuri. Now you have no guide.

You drive off, hunting aimlessly for the werewolves.

Go to 48.

31

With the WOW gun in one hand and the VCB in the other, you bring down many werewolves; but the creatures keep coming. Eventually you run out of ammunition, and the surviving werewolves leap forward, snarling.

He who fights and runs away, doesn't get turned into a werewolf today!

Go back to 1.

Yuri shrugs. "We wouldn't stand a chance on foot."

He drives towards a wooded island. Hundreds of werewolves in wolf and wolf-man form are gathered in a natural basin on its shore. Yuri stops the truck in their midst.

A gigantic wolf-man steps forward. "I am the Vurdalak."

You confront the werewolf leader. "We have come to offer peace."

The wolves' howls sound like mocking laughter.

"Your bravery amuses me," growls the Vurdalak. "I will let you go. But leave the truck."

To do as the Vurdalak says, go to 5.

To try to escape, go to 9.

33

You bring up your WOW gun but you are too slow. With a terrible snarl, a werewolf leaps from the shadows and pins you to the ground. Its powerful jaws tear into your throat.

You are paralysed as the were-virus in the creature's bite spreads through your body. You are becoming a werewolf!

Not the best way to end your mission! Go back to 1.

34

"We're here to stop a war!" Yuri tells the guards.

Reluctantly, they take you to the leader of their clan. The old werewolf appears in human form and listens carefully to what you say.

"You are right," he says heavily. "The wolfmoot will take place at the lake, on Olkhon Island, three hours before dawn. The Vurdalak will call for war and the clan leaders are not strong enough to stand against him."

As Yuri drives away, he checks his watch. "We must act fast."

You nod. "I have a plan..."

Go to 23.

35

The man calling to you shows all the classic signs of a werewolf in human form. You dodge him and go into the mill.

You find a row of cant hooks, used for handling logs, hanging beside the door. Taking one, you just have time to flatten yourself against the wall before your pursuer appears. He has shed his disguise to appear in wolf-man form.

You swing the cant hook, knocking him out cold. He lands on the carriage truck used to feed logs to the blade of the circular saw.

You hear movement outside.

To leave the wolf-man and investigate, go to 42.

To make sure the wolf-man is destroyed, go to 4.

The truck bounces to a halt in a clearing where a helicopter is waiting.

The helicopter clatters through the night, setting you down at an army base outside Irkutsk.

In the operations room, you are met by a general. "My orders are to make troops available and place them under your orders," he tells you, "but they will take twelve hours to assemble."

To wait for the troops, go to 48.

To deal with the werewolves yourself, go to 8.

37

You charge out of the hut to find the surviving wolf-men prowling outside, uncertain whether to renew their attack.

You chase them across the snow, seeking a clear shot. But as they disappear behind a hut, the floodlights around the compound go out.

It is very dark. You stalk after the werewolves, weapon at the ready; but you have only taken a dozen steps before you feel hot breath on your neck!

Go to 33.

38

Opening the box of charges Yuri has prepared, you hurl them at the werewolves.

The explosions blow many of the creatures sky-high and crack the ice. A great split in the frozen surface opens behind the truck. Paws scrabbling, unable to stop, your pursuers slide into it, plunging into the freezing waters with despairing howls. You breathe a sigh of relief. The cold will destroy the were-virus, killing the werewolves.

But then the truck lurches as the ice beneath it breaks. It crashes, and starts to sink. You glance into the cab. Yuri has cracked his head in the crash and is unconscious.

But as you reach out to help him, the Vurdalak appears — the last of your enemies, and the most deadly.

To fight the Vurdalak, go to 44.

To help Yuri, go to 12.

39

You follow the werewolf pack. But the wolves can move through the dense forest more quickly than a snowmobile.

Their trail leads you to a deserted logging camp. You check one of the huts. Inside, you find the bodies of several lumberjacks. The werewolves have been at work!

As you leave the hut, an apparent survivor of the massacre staggers towards you. But your HOWL detector reveals that this is no man, but a werewolf in human form!

To shoot the werewolf, go to 15.

To restrain him, go to 24.

40

"We don't have time!" you tell Yuri.

He scowls. "Then I will not help you."

You try to insist, but Yuri is adamant. In the end you have no choice but to search for the werewolves on your own.

The radio in the jeep keeps you in touch with Cranberry, but the information he has is vague. You have no idea where the wolfmoot might be.

Go to 48.

41

You raise your WOW weapon, switching on the gunlight fitting so that you can see your attackers. You take them all down.

But the noise of the shots has alerted the rest of the pack. The HOWL detector shows them racing towards you.

Go to 31.

42

You go to peer around the door, trying to see what is out there. But seconds later, you feel the creature's claws bite into your shoulder. You'd forgotten how quickly a werewolf can heal!

The wolf-man spins you round and lunges for your throat...

Never take your eyes off a wounded werewolf! Go back to 1.

43

"Those aren't wolves!" you cry. "They're werewolves!"

You take your WOW gun from your briefcase and start firing at the creatures, making every shot count. Soon, three werewolves lie dead in the snow, the were-virus that gave them unlife destroyed by the silver in your darts.

"Lunatic!" screams the professor. "Assassin!" He calls for his guards.

You ignore him and carry on shooting. But the guards arrive, firing as they run. Bullets slam into your body. You fall to the ground, your blood staining the snow.

You can't just blast away without explanation! Go back to 1.

44

You turn to face the Vurdalak.

Yuri's VCB and WOW were lost in the crash. All you have is your silver knife and a quiver of crossbow bolts — but nothing to fire them.

The Vurdalak pounces, snarling. Vicious claws tear into your arm, knocking the knife from your hand. The creature raises its other arm to deal your death-blow — and stops, puzzled, staring down at the feathered shaft sticking out of its hairy chest. You have stabbed it with a crossbow bolt tipped with wolfsbane.

With a howl of rage and despair, the creature staggers back and falls into the freezing waters. **Go to 50.**

45

You reach into your belt pouch and take out three silver ninja throwing stars. These bring down two attackers, but a third lashes at you with powerful claws, smashing your WOW gun. Another blow destroys your VCB. A punch to the head sends your comms link with Cranberry spinning away to be lost in the snow.

The wolf-man bares its teeth and goes for your throat — only to throw itself onto the silver knife you keep in your boot for such emergencies.

You check your HOWL detector. It, too, has been smashed in the struggle. You are blind and practically weaponless!

You stumble on until you spot the lights of a sawmill.

Go to 11.

46

"All right," you say, "but we must hurry."

You collect Yuri's G.H.O.S.T. equipment and he leads you to a battered Toyota 4x4 pickup. You notice that, in the back, there are several boxes carrying the international symbol for explosives.

"For blasting," Yuri explains.

"Are they safe?" you ask.

"Certainly — until they go off," he replies offhandedly.

You shrug and get in the truck. Yuri sets off for the nearest werewolf settlement.

But before you reach it, guards in wolf-man form intercept the truck. One snatches open the passenger door. "Get out!"

To ask the wolf-men for help, go to 34.

To fight them, go to 30.

47

You find Fedorov's living quarters and burst in.

"Professor," you cry, "the creatures you're sheltering are werewolves!"

Fedorov glares at you. "What madness is this?"

"They've replaced the real wolves. I'm guessing they're hiding out here while they test their strength. They must be destroyed!"

"You're insane!" snarls the professor. "Destroy my wolves? Never!"

Cranberry's voice comes over the comms link. "Has it occurred to you, Agent, that Fedorov might be a werewolf in human form? Do his eyebrows meet across the bridge of his nose? Are his fingernails long and curved? Are his ears set low, and pointed?"

"Well, he's no oil painting, that's for sure." You stare at the raging scientist.

To go after the werewolves yourself, go to 37.

To take Professor Fedorov prisoner, go to 22.

48

Hours pass. Suddenly the radio crackles as it picks up a frantic message from the city of Irkutsk. Your Russian is pretty rusty, but you understand a few words...

"We are under attack....werewolves...in the city...those who are bitten join their ranks...they are coming...they are here..." The broadcast ends with a high-pitched scream: then silence.

You put your head in your hands. You are too late. The truce between humans and werewolves is broken. There will be war — and who can say the werewolves will not win?

Go back to 1.

49

"We must attack!" you tell the colonel.

Borrowing an AK-74 assault rifle, you move stealthily to the door and glance outside. The yard around the mill is teeming with werewolves in both wolf and wolf-man form.

"Follow me!" you burst from the mill. The soldiers follow, firing round after round into the creatures.

But the werewolves heal so quickly from anything but silver and wolfsbane that the bullets have almost no effect. Soon you are forced to fall back.

To continue the fight, go to 14.

To break off and use the mill equipment instead, go to 29.

50

The following evening, Yuri has invited his friends and neighbours to a feast to celebrate the end of the werewolf threat. Cranberry is listening in via Yuri's comms link.

Yuri pats you on the shoulder. "And thank you, my friend, for saving my life."

He passes you a bowl of caviar and you take a generous helping.

"Don't wolf it," advises Cranberry.

EQUIPMENT

Ural Typhoon ATV: All Terrain Vehicle; Mine-Resistant Ambush Protected (MRAP), armoured personnel carrier.

Snowmobile: Designed to be operated on snow and ice where its skis and Kevlar tracks make it capable of speeds reaching more than 150 mph.

WOW (Works on Werewolves)

VCB (Very Cross Bow)

HOWL (Human or Werewolf Locator)

I HERO

MUTANT

STEVE BARLOW ◇ STEVE SKIDMORE

Illustrated by PAUL DAVIDSON

EDGE

You are an agent of **G.H.O.S.T.** — Global Headquarters Opposing Supernatural Threats.

You are based at Arcane Hall...Your butler, Cranberry, is another G.H.O.S.T. agent who assists you in your adventures.

Your life at Arcane Hall is comfortable and peaceful; but you know that at any moment, the G.H.O.S.T. High Command can order you into action in any part of the world...

You and Cranberry have been sent to Sydney, Australia. You are sitting in a café by the famous Opera House, waiting for the Director General of G.H.O.S.T. to contact you about the mission.

"Any idea why we are here?" you ask Cranberry.

Continue the adventure in:

About the 2Steves

"The 2Steves" are
Britain's most popular
writing double act
for young people,
specialising in comedy
and adventure. They
perform regularly in schools and libraries,
and at festivals, taking the power of words
and story to audiences of all ages.

Together they have written many books,
including the *I HERO Immortals* and *iHorror* series.

About the illustrator:
Paul Davidson

Paul Davidson is a British
illustrator and comic book artist.

I HERO Legends — collect them all!

ATHENA
978 1 4451 5234 9 pb
978 1 4451 5235 6 ebook

BEOWULF
978 1 4451 5225 7 pb
978 1 4451 5226 4 ebook

KING ARTHUR
978 1 4451 5231 8 pb
978 1 4451 5232 5 ebook

FREYA
978 1 4451 5237 0 pb
978 1 4451 5238 7 ebook

HERCULES
978 1 4451 5228 8 pb
978 1 4451 5229 5 ebook

ROBIN HOOD
978 1 4451 5183 0 pb
978 1 4451 5184 7 ebook

Have you read the I HERO Toons series?

INVASION OF THE BOTTY SNATCHERS
978 1 4451 5927 0 pb
978 1 4451 5928 7 ebook

ENTER THE PENGUIN
978 1 4451 5924 9 pb
978 1 4451 5925 6 ebook

KILLER CUSTARD
978 1 4451 5930 0 pb
978 1 4451 5931 7 ebook

KUNG FU KITTEN
978 1 4451 5918 8 pb
978 1 4451 5919 5 ebook

ROBIN HAMSTER
978 1 4451 5921 8 pb
978 1 4451 5922 5 ebook

ATTACK of the ZOMBIE BUNNIES
978 1 4451 5873 0 pb
978 1 4451 5874 7 ebook

978 1 4451 5104 5 pb
978 1 4451 5119 9 eBook

Immortals
HERO

Ninja
Steve Barlow - Steve Skidmore

You are a skilled, stealthy ninja.
Your village has been attacked by a
warlord called Raiden. Now YOU must
go to his castle and stop him before
he destroys more lives.

978 1 4451 5101 4 pb
978 1 4451 5117 5 eBook

Immortals
HERO

Warrior Princess
Steve Barlow - Steve Skidmore

You are the Warrior Princess.
Someone wants to steal the magical
ice diamonds from the Crystal
Caverns. YOU must discover who
it is and save your kingdom.

978 1 4451 5103 8 pb
978 1 4451 5121 2 eBook

Immortals
HERO

Unicorn
Steve Barlow - Steve Skidmore

You are a magical unicorn.
Empress Yin Yang has stolen Carmine,
the red unicorn. Yin Yang wants to
destroy the colourful Rainbow Land.
YOU must stop her!

978 1 4451 5102 1 pb
978 1 4451 5124 3 eBook

Immortals
HERO

Spy
Steve Barlow - Steve Skidmore

You are a spy, codenamed Scorpio.
Someone has taken control of secret
satellite laser weapons. YOU must find
out who is responsible and
stop their dastardly plans.